EMERALD TREE

First-Start® Legends

EMERALD TREE

A STORY FROM AFRICA

Retold by Janet Palazzo-Craig
Illustrated by Charles Reasoner

Troll

There once was
a princess with long,
beautiful hair.

Each day, the princess
marched about, so all
could admire her.

ne day, a bird appeared. "Good morning, princess," it said. "May I have a bit of your hair for my nest?"

"Never!" said the princess.

"You will be sorry," said the bird. Then it flew away.

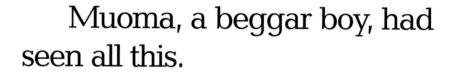

Muoma, a beggar boy, had
seen all this.

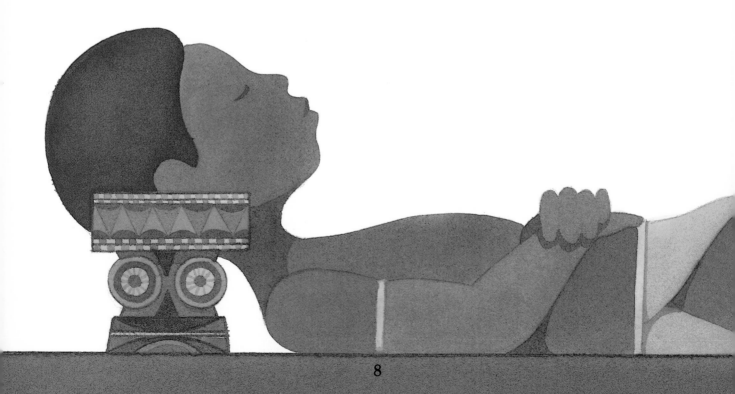

That night, Muoma had a
dream. In it, he chased the bird.
But it flew far away before he
could catch it.

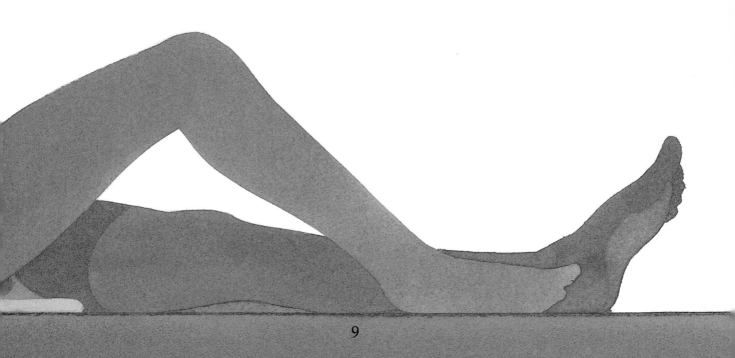

Time passed. A dry spell fell upon the land. Streams and rivers dried up. Leaves died and fell from the trees.

One day, a giant dust cloud swirled about the princess. When it passed, the princess's beautiful hair was gone!

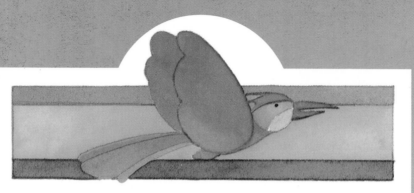

That night, Muoma had another dream. In it, he again saw the bird. As it flew, it dropped seeds. From the seeds grew trees full of fruit. From the fruit grew beautiful hair. When Muoma awoke, he knew what he must do.

The boy went to the king. "If you give me food and water for a journey, I will make your daughter's hair grow again." But the king would not listen.

Although he had
only a bit of water and
food, Muoma set off
on his journey. He
walked and walked
until morning. At last,
he stopped to eat.

Suddenly, many ants came up to him. "Can you feed us?" they asked.

The boy had little food, but he fed the ants.

Next, a flower spoke to him. "I am so dry."

"Here," said the boy, watering the flower.

Then a mouse appeared. "Please help me find my children," it said. "They are lost on the mountain."

Muoma was very tired, but he agreed to help.

t last, Muoma reached the mountaintop. Three beautiful trees stood before him. One was gold, one was silver, and one was emerald green.

With a flash, the golden tree changed into the bird from Muoma's dream. "Eat," said the bird. A feast was spread below the silver tree.

Muoma was about to eat when he remembered the mouse. "First, I must keep my promise," he said.

"Do not worry," said the bird. "I was the mouse, the ants, and the flower. I wanted to see if you were ready for a special gift."

The gift was a seed from
the emerald tree. A seed to
grow hair! The bird told the
boy to plant the seed in the
princess's garden.

Muoma did so. Each
night he watered the seed.
It began to grow into a tree.

All this time, the
princess had hidden away
in her room. One night,
she looked out and saw
Muoma by the tree.

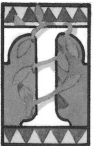he next night, Muoma was surprised to find that the plant had already been watered. He hid. Soon he heard the princess speak. "I will take care of you, beautiful tree," she said.

Muoma stepped out of the shadows. "You will soon be just as beautiful," he said.

Suddenly, a gust of wind blew the princess's veil from her head.

The princess's hair had grown back! Happily, Muoma and the princess danced and laughed.

By morning, the tree had grown tall. Birds sang and flew about it.

"I'll give them some of my hair for their nests!" said the princess. As she did so, rain began to fall!

The king and his people were full of joy. There was a great celebration to thank Muoma.

It came to pass that Muoma and the princess married. And for many years, they lived very happily, taking care of the singing birds and the emerald tree.

Emerald Tree is a legend of the Akamba people of East Africa. To these people, good weather means crops and animals will do well. But during a dry spell, such as the one in the story, all will suffer. Because the weather is so important to them, the Akamba people create songs, dances, and stories such as this one about it.

Like many legends throughout the world, this story has a hero who goes on a long journey, accomplishes a good deed, and proves himself worthy of great praise.